CARTER HIGH
M Y S T E R I E S

ART SHOW
Mystery

By Eleanor Robins

SADDLEBACK
EDUCATIONAL PUBLISHING

CARTER HIGH
M Y S T E R I E S

Art Show Mystery   Lucky Falcon Mystery
Aztec Ring Mystery   The Missing Test Mystery
Drama Club Mystery   The Secret Admirer Mystery
The Field Trip Mystery   The Secret Message
Library Book Mystery   Where Is Mr. Zane?

www.sdlback.com

ISBN-13: 978-1-61651-560-7
ISBN-10: 1-61651-560-0
eBook: 978-1-61247-128-0

Printed in Guangzhou, China
NOR/0713/CA21301351

17 16 15 14 13   3 4 5 6 7

Chapter 1

It was Monday. Paige was on her way to art class. Miss Brock was her art teacher.

Logan walked with Paige. He was in the class, too.

Paige and Logan were good friends. They both lived at Grayson Apartments. And they rode the same bus to school.

"Did you finish your painting, Logan?" Paige asked.

"No. But I will today," Logan said.

"I hope I can finish my painting today," Paige said.

But she wasn't sure she would. She

wanted to do a lot more to it.

"I want to put my painting in the art show," Paige said.

The art show was this Friday.

"What about you, Logan? Are you going to put your painting in the art show?" Paige asked.

"Not me. I don't want people to talk about my painting," Logan said.

Paige didn't know why Logan felt that way. She wanted people to look at her painting. And she wanted them to talk about it, too.

Paige and Logan got to the art room. They went into the room.

The bell rang. It was time for class to start.

Miss Brock said, "All of you need to work hard. The art show is this Friday. Try to finish your paintings today. Then we can start to get ready for the art show tomorrow."

Logan asked, "Do I have to put my painting in the art show?"

"No, Logan. But I hope you'll put your work in the show. I hope all of you do," Miss Brock said.

But Paige didn't think Logan would.

Paige put her books down. She walked over to her painting. It was next to Skye's painting.

Paige looked at Skye's painting.

Paige said, "I like your painting."

"Thanks," Skye said.

But Skye didn't say that she liked Paige's painting.

Paige picked up her paintbrush. She was ready to work on her painting.

Miss Brock said, "Time to start. Work hard."

Paige worked on her painting for a long time.

Then Miss Brock said, "You need to save some time to clean up. So you have only ten more minutes to work."

Paige thought her painting was good. She hoped Miss Brock would think it was, too.

Miss Brock asked, "Have you finished your painting, Paige?"

"Not yet, Miss Brock," Paige said.

Miss Brock walked over to Paige. She looked at Paige's painting.

Then she said, "I like your painting, Paige. It's very nice."

"Thank you, Miss Brock," she said.

Paige was glad Miss Brock liked her painting. She hoped other people would, too.

Miss Brock said, "I hope you put your painting in the art show, Paige.

Then everyone can see it."

"Oh, yes, Miss Brock. I sure will," Paige said.

Maybe she would win a prize, too. That would be great.

Chapter 2

It was the next day. Paige was on her way to art class. Logan walked with her.

"I hope I finish my painting today," Paige said.

"Do you still want to put it in the art show?" Logan asked.

Paige said, "Yes. I hope I can win a prize. You've seen my painting, Logan. Do you think I can win a prize?"

Logan stopped to talk to Mr. Nash. And he didn't answer Paige.

Paige stopped to talk to Mr. Nash, too.

Mr. Nash cleaned the school. And sometimes he fixed things.

Mr. Nash was in the classroom next to the art room. He'd just put new numbers on the door.

Logan asked, "Why did you put new numbers on the door, Mr. Nash?"

"Mr. Glenn told me to do it."

Mr. Glenn was the principal.

"What about the other doors? Are you going to put new numbers on them, too?" Logan asked.

"Maybe I will. Maybe Mr. Ross will," Mr. Nash said.

Mr. Ross worked at the school, too.

Logan said, "The old numbers are okay. Why does Mr. Glenn want to change them?"

"Don't ask me. Ask Mr. Glenn," Mr. Nash said.

"The new numbers look better than the old numbers," Paige said.

"But the old numbers were okay.

So why change them?" Logan asked.

The bell rang. Paige and Logan hurried into the art room. It was time for class to start.

Miss Brock said, "A few of you still need to finish your artwork. And you need to do it quickly."

"Why?" Logan asked.

Miss Brock said, "Mr. Glenn came to see your artwork this morning. He said your artwork is very good. And he said all of your artwork must be moved to room 19."

That surprised Paige. She thought the art show would be in the art room.

Logan said, "Why do we have to move our artwork? I thought the show would be in here."

Miss Brock said, "It will be. But Mr. Glenn wants everything moved out of here. Then Mr. Nash and Mr. Ross can clean the room."

"When will they clean the room?" Paige asked.

Miss Brock said, "They'll clean the room tomorrow. So we'll meet in room 127. Then on Thursday, you can begin to move your artwork back in here. And we'll get ready for the art show."

"When do you want us to move our artwork today?" Paige asked.

Miss Brock said, "I hope you can take it to room 19 before art class is over."

Logan said, "I don't want my work in the art show. Can I take it home today? Or do you want me to take it to room 19?"

Logan's painting wasn't very big. So he could take it home on the bus.

"I'll grade it today, Logan. Then you can take it home," Miss Brock said.

Miss Brock told two boys to take their artwork to room 19. She gave one of them a key to the door.

Miss Brock said, "Put your artwork in there. Then lock the door. And bring the key back to me."

Paige worked on her painting.

It wasn't long until the two boys were back. More students moved their artwork. And time went by quickly.

At last, the painting was finished. Paige thought it was very good.

Skye walked over to Paige. She looked at the painting.

Skye asked, "Did you finish your painting, Paige?"

"Yes," Paige said.

"Are you going to put it in the art show?" Skye asked.

"Yes. I hope that I win a prize," Paige said.

"I wouldn't count on it," Skye said.

Paige quickly put the paint away. And she cleaned her paintbrush. Then she was ready to take her painting to room 19.

Why did Skye say that? Paige wanted to ask her. But the bell rang. It was time for the end of class.

Paige needed to go to her next class. It was too late to take her painting to room 19. She went over to Miss Brock.

Paige said, "I don't have time to take my painting to room 19. What am I going to do?"

"Come by my room some time today. And you can take your painting then. You can borrow my key to room 19," Miss Brock said.

But Paige didn't have any free time for the rest of the day. She had a math test. And she had to study for it. She was going to do that at lunch. So she couldn't take her painting then.

When would she have time to take her painting to room 19?

Chapter 3

Paige was in her math class. Mr. Hwang was her teacher.

Paige worked hard on her math test. She wanted to finish early. Then maybe Mr. Hwang would let her go to the art class. And she could take her painting to room 19.

Paige finished the math test. Then she checked her answers. She thought she'd done a good job on the test. She took the test to Mr. Hwang.

"Is it okay for me to leave early? I have to go to the art room. I need to get my painting. And I have to take it to room 19," Paige said.

Mr. Hwang knew about the art show. And he knew the students had to move their artwork.

"Did you check your answers, Paige?" Mr. Hwang asked.

Paige said, "Yes, Mr. Hwang. And I think I did well on my test."

"Then you can go, Paige. But take all of your books with you," he said.

"Thanks, Mr. Hwang," Paige said.

Paige got her books. And she hurried to the art room. She knew she didn't have much time.

Paige saw Mr. Nash. He was sweeping the floor outside the art room.

"Hi, Mr. Nash," Paige said.

Then Paige went into the art room. Most of the artwork was gone. But not all of it.

Paige looked for Miss Brock. But it

was her planning time. And Miss Brock wasn't there. So Paige couldn't borrow her key.

Paige went back into the hall. She walked over to Mr. Nash.

"Do you know where Miss Brock is?" Paige asked.

Maybe Miss Brock was somewhere nearby. Then Paige could get the key.

"I don't know," Mr. Nash said.

"I need to take my painting to room 19. And the room is locked. Miss Brock said I could borrow her key. But she isn't here. So I can't get her key. Can I borrow your keys?" Paige asked.

Mr. Nash had many keys on a key ring.

"Sorry, I can't let you do that," Mr. Nash said.

"But I'll bring them right back. And I won't unlock any other room," Paige said.

"I can't let you borrow them. Or I would

have to let all of the students borrow them. I sure can't do that," Mr. Nash said.

What was Paige going to do? She had to move her painting. And this was the only time she had to do it.

Mr. Nash said, "Tell you what I'll do. I'll go with you. And I'll unlock the door for you."

"Thanks, Mr. Nash. That's very nice of you," Paige said.

Paige hurried back into the art room. She got her painting. Then she went out into the hall. It was hard to carry both her painting and her books.

"Need some help? I'd be glad to carry the painting for you," Mr. Nash said.

"Thanks," Paige said. She gave the painting to Mr. Nash.

The two quickly went down the hall to room 19.

Paige saw Mr. Ross. He had just put

new numbers on one of the doors. Some doors already had new numbers.

Paige saw room 19. New numbers were on the door. Paige stopped and looked at the door.

"This is the room," Paige said.

"Are you sure this is the right room?" Mr. Nash asked.

"Yes," Paige said.

"Are you really sure about that?" Mr. Nash asked.

Paige said, "Yes. This is the room Miss Brock said to put it in."

Mr. Nash put the painting on the floor. He unlocked the door. Then he took the painting into the room.

Mr. Nash asked, "Where do you want me to put your painting?"

Paige showed him where to put the painting. And Mr. Nash put it there.

Then the two of them went out into

the hall. And Mr. Nash locked the door.

"Thanks for the help, Mr. Nash," Paige said.

Then Paige hurried to her next class. She didn't want to be late.

Her painting was in room 19 now. And she didn't have to worry any more about it.

Chapter 4

It was Thursday. Paige hurried into the art room. Logan was already there. It was almost time for art class to start.

"The art room looks very nice, Miss Brock," Paige said.

The floor was very clean. The tables had white tablecloths on them. Some tables had artwork on them, too.

The bell rang.

Miss Brock said, "You can help me get ready for the art show. Or you can draw or use this class as a study time."

Paige wanted to help Miss Brock get ready for the art show.

Miss Brock said, "You can go to room 19. Two at a time. Get your artwork and bring it back here. Be quiet on the way. And don't forget, lock the room when you leave."

Miss Brock picked two students to go to room 19 first. She gave one of them her key to the room.

Paige looked at Logan.

Paige asked, "What are you going to do, Logan?"

"I need to study. So I guess I'll study," Logan said.

"I'll help Miss Brock," Paige said.

"Who wants to help me get ready for the show?" Miss Brock asked.

"I do," Paige said.

"So do I," Skye said.

Some other students said they wanted to help, too.

Paige started to help Miss Brock.

Other students went to get their artwork, two at a time.

The time went by quickly.

Then Miss Brock said, "Paige, you need to get your artwork. And you need to hurry. It's almost time for class to be done. Skye, you go with Paige."

Miss Brock gave Skye the key to unlock the door.

Paige and Skye went out into the hall. They were the last two to get their artwork. They started to walk quickly to room 19.

They got to the hallway where room 19 was located. Skye stopped in front of a door.

Skye said, "Good, we're here."

Paige was surprised. She didn't think she and Mr. Nash put her painting in this room.

"Are you sure this is the room?" Paige asked.

Skye said, "Yes. I put my painting in this room. Look on the door. And you'll see this is the right room."

Paige looked at the numbers on the door. They were one and nine. So it must be the right room.

Skye unlocked the door.

Paige and Skye went into the room.

Paige said, "This doesn't look like the right room to me."

"It does to me. You just forgot where you put your painting," Skye said.

But how could Paige forget where she put her painting? Some of the artwork was back in the art room. Maybe that was why the room didn't look the same to her.

Skye hurried over to her painting. She picked it up.

Then Skye said, "We need to get back to class. So hurry and get your painting, Paige."

Paige looked at where she thought her painting would be.

But her painting wasn't there. Had someone moved it?

Chapter 5

Paige walked around the room. Only a few paintings were in the room. She looked at all of them.

Her painting had to be there. But it wasn't there.

Skye said, "I have my painting. Hurry and get your painting, Paige. We need to go back to the art room. It's almost time for our next class."

"My painting is gone," Paige said.

Skye didn't look surprised that Paige said that.

"Are you sure?" Skye asked.

"Yes. I'm sure," Paige said.

"Did you look at all of the paintings?" Skye asked.

"Yes," Paige said.

"Are you sure you put your painting in here? Maybe you did put it in some other room," Skye said.

"I put it in room 19. And this is room 19," Paige said.

"Maybe Miss Brock knows where it is," Skye said.

Miss Brock sent Paige to room 19 to get the painting. So Paige didn't think Miss Brock knew where it was.

But maybe Miss Brock did know. And she just forgot to tell Paige.

"Maybe you should look some more in here. But we need to get back to the art room. We can't be late to our next class," Skye said.

Paige didn't want to go to her next class. She wanted to look for her painting.

But she didn't know where to look for it. It wasn't in room 19. She was sure about that.

The girls went out to the hall. Skye had her painting. So Paige locked the door.

The bell rang.

Paige and Skye walked quickly.

When they got back to the art room, Logan and most of the other students had gone.

Skye put her painting on a table.

Miss Brock asked, "Where's your painting, Paige?"

"It wasn't in room 19. And I don't know where it is. Do you know where it is?" Paige asked.

"No, Paige. Are you sure it wasn't in room 19?" Miss Brock asked.

"Yes," Paige said.

"Skye, did you help Paige look for it?" Miss Brock asked.

Skye said, "No, Miss Brock. We had to hurry back here. So I didn't have time to help Paige."

But Skye didn't need to help her look. The painting wasn't in room 19.

"Where could it be, Miss Brock?" Paige asked.

"I don't know, Paige," she said.

"Do you think someone moved it?" Paige asked.

"No, Paige. I don't know how someone could have moved it. The room was locked. And the person would need a key," Miss Brock said.

But most of the students in Paige's class had been to room 19. The students in some other art classes had been there, too. They all had a key to unlock the door, so they could get their own work.

Did someone in her class take the

painting? Or did someone in one of the other classes take it?

But why?

Paige needed to go to her next class. So she went to get her books. Skye went to get her books, too.

Skye said, "I'm sure you'll find your painting, Paige. But it might be after the art show."

Then Skye hurried out of the room.

Why did Skye say that? Did she take the painting? But why? Was it because she thought Paige might win a prize?

Maybe Skye did take the painting. But when did Skye take it? And where did Skye put Paige's painting?

Chapter 6

It was lunchtime. Paige hurried into the lunchroom. She was still very upset. She quickly got her lunch. Then she looked for her friends.

Paige saw Logan. Logan was at a table with Drake, Jack, Lin, and Willow. Paige hurried over to their table and sat down.

Logan said, "You don't look so good, Paige. What's wrong with you?"

"Yeah. What's wrong with you?" Drake asked.

"My painting is missing," Paige said.

"Are you sure?" Lin asked.

"Yes. Do you think someone took it?" Paige asked.

Paige thought Skye took it. But she didn't know that for sure. So she didn't want to say anything.

Logan laughed.

"Why did you laugh? It isn't funny," Paige said.

"Sorry, I couldn't help it. I have seen your painting. And believe me about this, Paige. No one would steal it. It isn't that good," Logan said.

"That wasn't nice, Logan," Willow said.

"For sure," Jack said.

"Sorry, but it's true," Logan said.

"Okay, so maybe you don't like my painting. But Miss Brock said it's very nice," Paige said.

Logan laughed again. Then he said, "Sorry, I couldn't help it, Paige."

"Now what's so funny?" she asked.

"Miss Brock tells all the students their artwork is nice. She even says that to me. And you know how bad my artwork is," Logan said.

"Logan's teasing you, Paige. Don't let him upset you," Willow said.

Willow was being nice. But Paige knew Logan wasn't joking. That's what he really thought.

Maybe her painting wasn't that good. And maybe she wouldn't win a prize in the show. And maybe Skye didn't take her painting after all. But where was her painting?

Lin asked, "How do you know the painting is gone, Paige? Did Miss Brock say it is?"

"No. She sent me to get it. And I couldn't find it. It was gone," Paige said.

"Maybe you didn't look in the right room for it," Drake said.

Jack said, "Yeah, maybe you didn't look in the right room for it."

"I put my painting in room 19. So it had to be in that room," Paige said.

"Maybe someone moved your painting," Logan said.

"Someone moved it," Jack said.

"But where is it?" Paige asked.

"Don't worry, Paige. We'll help you find it," Willow said.

"Yes, Paige. We'll help you find it," Lin said.

"For sure," Jack said.

Willow looked at Logan and Drake.

Then Willow said, "All of us will help."

"Yes, all of us," Drake said.

"Yeah," said Logan.

They were her friends. So Paige was sure that they would help her solve the mystery. But could they help her find her painting before the art show?

Chapter 7

Paige tried to eat. But she kept thinking about her painting.

"Cheer up, Paige. It's only a lost painting," Logan said.

"That wasn't nice, Logan. The painting means a lot to Paige. And we have to find it," Willow said.

"What can I do to help? Just say the word. And I'll do it," Jack said.

Paige said, "I don't know. I just know we have to find my painting."

"We can ask around. Maybe someone has seen it," Drake said.

"But the art show is tomorrow," Paige said.

Lin said, "I wish we could all look for the painting. But we can't do it now. And we have to ride the bus home. So we can't stay after school."

"Just say the word. And I'll take you home," Jack said.

Jack was the only one who had a car. It wasn't much of a car. But it was still a car. Jack liked to show it off. So he was always glad to take them somewhere.

"How, Jack? You don't have your car at school," Logan said.

"I'll ride the bus home. Then I'll come back in my car. And I'll take you home," Jack said.

"Great idea, Jack," Willow said.

"That sounds like a plan," Drake said.

"Thanks, Jack. It's very nice of you to do that," Paige said.

"Where should we meet after school?" Lin asked.

"Let's meet outside the art room," Paige said.

Paige thought that was the best place to meet. Then she could talk to Miss Brock. Maybe Miss Brock had heard something about her painting.

Willow said, "Just one thing. I have to work today. So I can't stay after school."

Willow wanted to be a librarian. So she worked at the town library some days after school and some weekends.

Drake said, "I have football practice. And you know I can't be late to that. So I can't help after school."

Drake was on the football team. He was the quarterback.

"But Logan and I can still help, right Logan?" Lin asked. Lin looked hopefully at Logan.

"Right," Logan said. "I guess I can help."

Chapter 8

Paige was in her last class of the day. Jack was in the class, too.

The end of school bell rang.

Paige was glad. Now she could look for her painting.

Jack came over to Paige.

Jack said, "I'll be back as soon as I can."

"Thanks, Jack. But don't drive too fast," Paige said.

"Never," Jack said.

Paige believed him. He cared too much about his car to drive too fast.

Jack hurried out of the classroom.

Paige quickly picked up her books. Then she hurried to the art room.

Logan and Lin were waiting for her outside the door.

"What should we do first, Paige?" Logan asked.

"We should talk to Miss Brock. Maybe she's heard something about my painting," Paige said.

They went into the art room. The room was almost ready for the art show.

"Look at the great artwork, Logan," Lin said.

"Yeah," said Logan. "And look how clean the art room is."

Paige saw Miss Brock. "Have you found my painting, Miss Brock? Or have you heard something about it?" she asked.

Miss Brock said, "No, Paige. But maybe it's in room 19. And you just didn't see it. Maybe you should look there again."

"Good idea," Logan said.

Did Logan think the painting was there? Did he think she didn't know her own painting?

"I have a key to the room, Paige. You can borrow it," Miss Brock said.

Miss Brock gave the key to Paige.

Paige said, "Thanks, Miss Brock. I'll bring it back as soon as I can."

Then Paige hurried to room 19. Logan and Lin were with her.

"I know my painting isn't in there. I've already looked there," Paige said.

"It won't hurt to look again, Paige," Lin said.

Paige unlocked the door. And they went in. Some artwork was in the room. But not very much.

The three looked around the room. But they didn't see Paige's painting.

"Are you sure you put your painting in here?" Logan asked.

Paige was starting to get very mad at Logan.

"I put my painting in room 19," Paige said. "And this is room 19."

Logan walked out into the hall. He looked at the room number.

Then he said, "Yeah, it sure is. But maybe you didn't put your painting in room 19 after all."

"I did," Paige almost yelled at Logan.

Paige looked down the hall. She saw Mr. Nash.

"You can ask Mr. Nash. He unlocked the door for me. And he put my painting in the room. He can tell you it was room

19," Paige said.

"Okay," Logan said. "I'll ask him."

Paige just said that to Logan. She didn't think he would ask Mr. Nash.

Logan walked over to Mr. Nash. Paige and Lin did, too.

Paige said, "You unlocked the door for me, Mr. Nash. And you put my painting in the room. It was room 19, right?"

"It sure was," Mr. Nash said.

Paige looked at Logan. She said, "I told you it was."

"That day it was," Mr. Nash said.

"What does that mean, Mr. Nash?" Logan asked.

"That day it was room 19. Today it's room 15," Mr. Nash said.

Paige couldn't believe what Mr. Nash had just said.

"How could that be?" Paige asked.

"Mr. Ross put the wrong numbers on some of the doors. I had to change them this morning," Mr. Nash said.

"That's why you can't find your painting. It's in room 15," Logan said.

Logan started to laugh.

Mr. Nash said, "I'll unlock room 15 for you. Your painting should be in there. That's the room we put it in."

Mr. Nash went to room 15. Paige and Logan went with him. Lin did, too. Mr. Nash unlocked the door.

Paige hurried into the room. She quickly found her missing painting. It hadn't been missing after all.

"Great, Paige. It's here," Lin said.

The painting might not win a prize. But Paige was glad she found it.

Paige looked at Logan. He was

laughing again.

"Okay, Logan. I was wrong this time. But that's the only time I was wrong," Paige said.

Then she started to laugh, too.